D0490593

THIS WALKER BOOK BELONGS TO:

_____

_____

_____

_____

For THAT GOOD MOTHER-IN-LAW
M.W.

First published 1990 by
Walker Books Ltd, 87 Vauxhall Walk
London SE11 5HJ

This edition published 1997

2 4 6 8 10 9 7 5 3

Text © 1990 Martin Waddell
Illustrations © 1990 Charlotte Voake
Cover illustration © 1997 Charlotte Voake

Printed in Hong Kong

British Library Cataloguing in Publication Data
A catalogue record for this book is available
from the British Library.

ISBN 0-7445-5227-3

AMY SAID

Written by Martin Waddell
Illustrated by Charlotte Voake

WALKER BOOKS
AND SUBSIDIARIES
LONDON • BOSTON • SYDNEY

When Amy and I stayed with Gran,

I wanted to bounce on my bed

and Amy said I could.

I just bounced a bit,

then a bit more,

then a bit more.

Then I fell off the bed. And Amy said...

we could *swing* instead.

"Gran's curtains are fun,"
Amy said.

And she swung

and she crashed

and she bashed Gran's chair.

It was all *my* fault, Amy said.

Gran gave us sausage and beans.

"Mug likes sausage and beans," Amy said.

So I gave mine to Mug.

And Mug mucked them

all over the floor.

Amy said perhaps Gran wouldn't see

because Gran was making me...

a Monster Head!

Amy said it was a Green Gobbler.

And Amy drew pictures

in green and red

to say thank you to Gran

for making my head.

Then Amy said,

"The walls need painting now."

So I painted them green

like my Gobbler.

And Mug came

and Mug did it *again.*

Then Amy said...

we'd give milk to Gran's cat

for being so good

and not making messes like Mug.

But as well as the milk,

Gran's cat

took Gran's fish

from Gran's dish.

And Amy said...

we should pick

Gran some flowers

in case she was cross.

We picked ALL of the flowers

 in Gran's garden.

I don't think she was cross

because ...

she gave us a party

with cakes and with buns

and with jelly and friends.

And Amy said
the jelly was smelly,
so I kicked it.

Then our friends went home
and Amy and I made a bike track
for Gran in her garden.

I rode my bike

and Amy dug bits.

And Amy went

SPLOSH

in the mud!

Gran *never* gets cross!

She put us both in the bath and

the water was lovely and warm.

We splashed just a bit, but the bit

splashed out on Gran's floor.

And Gran said...

"NO MORE!"

Then she helped us get dry and she said we should try to be good.

And Amy said

that we would,

because we love our Gran...

and we want to come back

again and again and again.

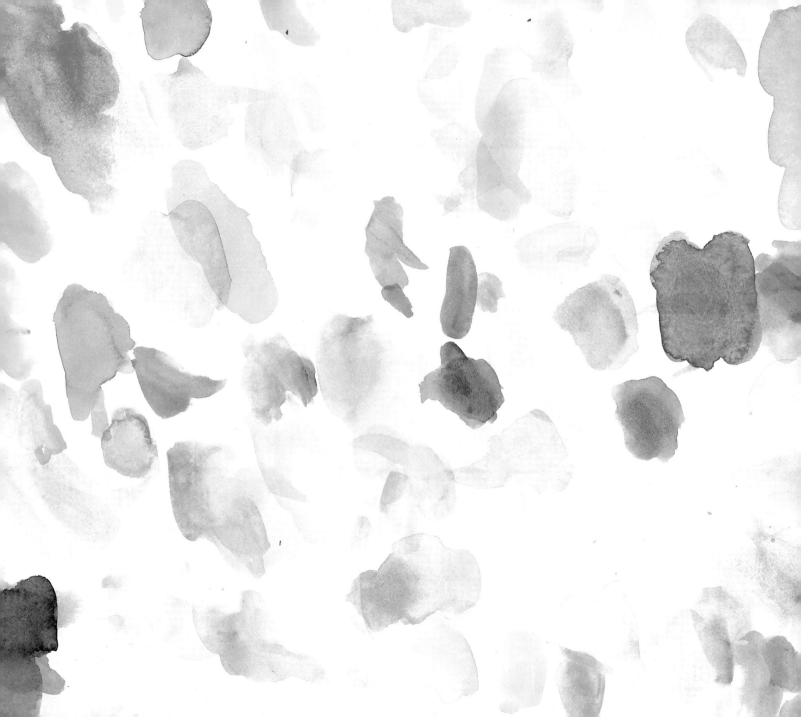

3 8002 01164 7379

MORE WALKER PAPERBACKS
For You to Enjoy

WE LOVE THEM
by Martin Waddell/Penny Dale

Two children and their dog, Ben, find a lost rabbit in the snow.
Ben and the rabbit become great friends. But Ben is growing old...

"Introduces death naturally and matter-of-factly and
makes every word tell." *Susan Hill, The Sunday Times*

0-7445-1774-5   £4.50

ONCE THERE WERE GIANTS
by Martin Waddell/Penny Dale

The story of a girl's development from infancy to motherhood.

"Deeply satisfying to read and reread ... delicately-drawn,
nicely realistic domestic scenes." *The Observer*

0-7445-1791-5   £4.99

MRS GOOSE'S BABY
by Charlotte Voake

Shortlisted for the Best Book for Babies Award

There's something very strange about Mrs Goose's baby - but her
mother love is so great that she alone cannot see what it is!

"An ideal picture book for the youngest child." *The Good Book Guide*

0-7445-4791-1   £4.99

Walker Paperbacks are available from most booksellers, or by post from B.B.C.S., P.O. Box 941, Hull, North Humberside HU1 3YQ
24 hour telephone credit card line 01482 224626

To order, send: Title, author, ISBN number and price for each book ordered, your full name and address,
cheque or postal order payable to BBCS for the total amount and allow the following for postage and packing:
UK and BFPO: £1.00 for the first book, and 50p for each additional book to a maximum of £3.50.
Overseas and Eire: £2.00 for the first book, £1.00 for the second and 50p for each additional book.
Prices and availability are subject to change without notice.